2021 Lawrence, Kansas

ISBN Number: 978-0-578-90279-1 (Paperback)

Library of Congress Control Number: 2021908117

jbookswithsmiles@gmail.com

alne

By Jessica A. Brown

He sat there on the classroom carpet.

Colors vanished and everything turned into a grey blur.

Noises swirled in the air, yet they did not enter his ears.

He sat there with other children around him.

But he felt

alone.

The children were kind.

They were energetic.

They would say, "Hello!"

But he didn't talk to them.

He sat there in silence.

In his own world.

In his own shell.

His head

was full of thoughts.

Until suddenly...

He noticed something.

On the floor by the classroom trashcan, there was something flat.

For a second, he even thought he heard something.

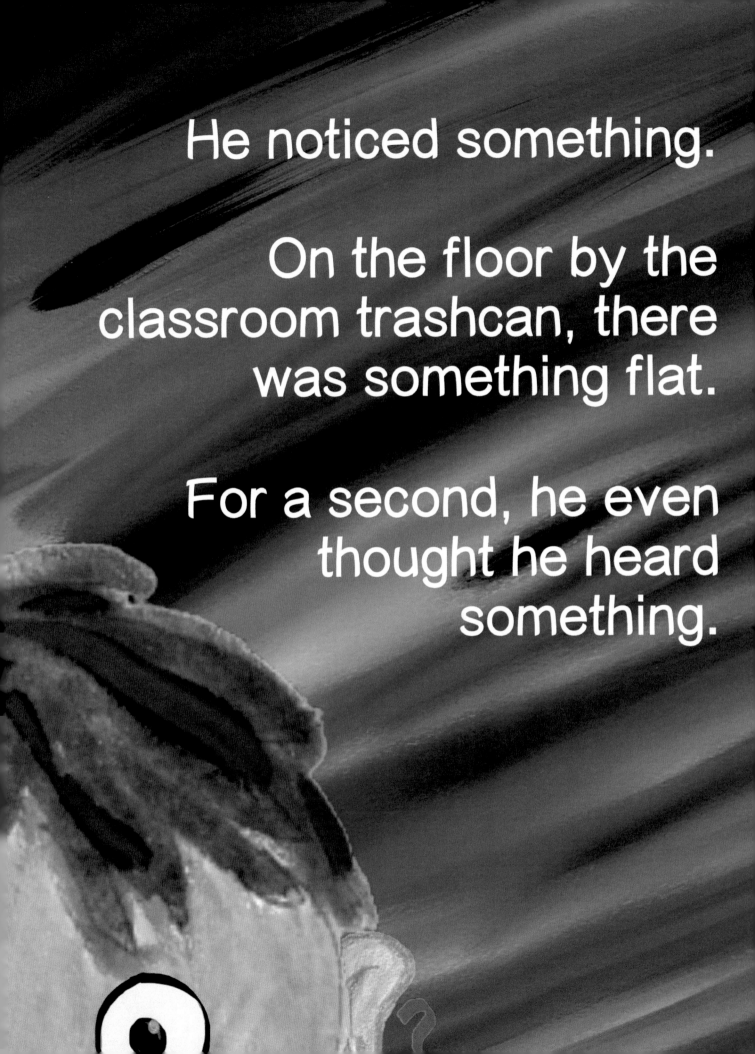

Without anyone seeing, he stepped away from the blur and snatched that flat thing. The thing he noticed was now his. He could hear it crinkle. He could feel how soft it was.

Despite the *whirling* blur around him,

he finally felt connected to something.

He stuffed
it in his
backpack.

It was his
and only his.

He began to see hints of

color in the grey blur.

Over and over,
he noticed
little things.

He came out of the whirling blur to explore and collect them.

He found a red thing.
A **black** thing.
A small thing.
A l o n g thing.

They were his things. They found a place in his heart, and they struck an idea in his head. He put them in his backpack then he faded back into the blur.

He gathered his collection of things.

He twisted, colored, cut, and glued. He added eyes, a nose, a mouth. He finished it off with a red bowtie.

All the little things became something bigger and better. A friend!

One day on the classroom carpet, he lifted his head and saw the other children looking at him with bright eyes!

Had they always done this?
How had he missed this?

His heart skipped a beat. His tummy felt funny.

He saw faces. He felt the cool air around him. He noticed beautiful colors. For the first time, he did not feel alone.

A smile caught his eye. He turned and saw another. All of the children had sparkling smiles just for him. Then he heard two small words,

"Hello there!"

He gulped. His eyes opened wide. He grinned hesitantly. He took a deep breath and said,

"Thinking," he said nervously.
"Thinking about what?" the voice replied.

"Mr. Bag!"

he exclaimed with excitement.

"Mr. What?!"

several voices echoed back with giggles.

He *dashed* to his cubby and *reached* into his backpack. He *clung* to the friend he made, and he slowly *walked* back to the colorful carpet.

"This ..." he *muttered* softly, "This is Mr. Bag! He is my friend. He hears me when I talk to him. He sees me when I am there. Mr. Bag likes to play and laugh. I think about him a lot."

"Hello,
Mr. Bag!"
all the
voices said
at once.

He then realized that Mr. Bag was not his only friend. These children were his friends too. They were there all along, but he hadn't noticed.

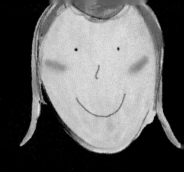

From that moment on, he felt *seen*. His voice was *heard*. He was finally *connected*. He was filled with love from Mr. Bag and his new friends. There was power in noticing. He was no longer

alone.

-143 ♡

About the Author

Jessica A. Brown is a First Grade teacher from Lawrence, Kansas. She has her Masters in Curriculum and Instruction with an emphasis in Teacher Leadership from Emporia State University. Jessica is a proud alumnae of Alpha Sigma Alpha Sorority, Epsilon Epsilon chapter. When she is not teaching, or writing lesson plans, she enjoys spending time with her friends and family at local restaurants or events. Her favorite place is being out on the water at Table Rock Lake. Jessica can be found on Instagram and Facebook with the username @jbookswithsmiles. She can also be found on Twitter with the handle @seek2teach1. (Like, follow and tag her!)

Made in the USA
Las Vegas, NV
28 April 2021